Mother's Mother's Day

by

Lorna Balian

Star Bright Books
New York

Published in the United States of America by Star Bright Books, Inc., New
York. The name Star Bright Books and the Star Bright Books logo are
registered trademarks of Star Bright Books, Inc.
Please visit www.starbrightbooks.com.

ISBN 1-932065-39-3

Printed in China
9   8   7   6   5   4   3   2   1

                    Library of Congress Cataloging-in-Publication Data

Balian, Lorna.
   Mother's Mother's Day / Lorna Balian.
        p. cm.
   Summary: Hazel the mouse goes to visit her mother on Mother's Day, but
finds she has gone to visit her mother.
   ISBN 1-932065-39-3
   [1. Mice--Fiction. 2. Mother's Day--Fiction.] I. Title.
PZ7.B1978 Mo 2004
[E]--dc22
                                        2003022427

For Mary Ann

Hazel went to visit her mother.
It was a special day,
and she was taking her
a beautiful bouquet of violets.

But Mother wasn't home! Tsk!

Mother had gone to visit her mother.
Because it was such a special day,
she was taking her a big, plump acorn.

But Grandmother wasn't home! Tsk! Tsk!

Grandmother had gone to visit *her* mother.
Because it was such a very special day,
she was taking her a ripe, wild strawberry.

But Great-Grandmother wasn't home!
Tsk! Tsk! Tsk!

Great-grandmother had gone to visit *her* mother. Because it was such a very, very special day, she was taking her some kernels of popcorn.

But Great-Great-Grandmother wasn't home!
Tsk! Tsk! Tsk! Tsk!

Great-Great-Grandmother had gone to visit *her* mother. Because it was such a very, very, very special day, she was taking her some soft feathers for her bed.

But Great-Great-Great-Grandmother
was not home!

Great-Great-Great-Grandmother
had gone to visit Hazel.

"Well, Happy Mother's Day, everyone!" squeaked Hazel.